TROUBLE at TABLE 5

#5:
Trouble to the Max

Check out all the
TROUBLE at TABLE 5
books!

#1   #2   #3   #4   #5

Read more books by **Tom Watson**

#1-12   #1-5

HARPER Chapters

TROUBLE at TABLE 5

#5:
Trouble to the Max

by **Tom Watson**

illustrated by
Marta Kissi

HARPER
An Imprint of HarperCollinsPublishers

Dedicated to Jacob
(IASPOWYA)

Trouble at Table 5 #5: Trouble to the Max
Text copyright © 2021 by Tom Watson
Illustrations copyright © 2021 by HarperCollins Publishers
Illustrations by Marta Kissi

Library of Congress Control Number: 2020950509
ISBN 978-0-06-300450-4 — ISBN 978-0-06-300449-8 (paperback)

Typography by Torberg Davern
21 22 23 24 25   PC/LSCC   10 9 8 7 6 5 4 3 2 1

First Edition

Table of Contents

CHAPTER ONE
MR. WILLOW BITES HIS FINGER

WE HAD ONLY been in our seats for a couple of minutes on Monday morning when Mr. Willow called from the front of the classroom, "Table 5!"

"What did we do?" Simon whispered to Rosie and me. "We just got here."

"We didn't do anything," Rosie said quietly back. She giggled a little. "I love how you're already assuming that we're in trouble."

Simon shrugged and said, "It's in my nature."

Since those two were whispering back and forth, I figured I better answer our teacher.

"Yes, Mr. Willow?" I called back.

"Molly, will you three come up here?" he said and opened a manila folder. He took out a stack of papers. "You can help me pass out these math quizzes."

While our classmates quietly complained, Rosie, Simon, and I headed toward Mr. Willow.

"That's enough moaning and groaning," Mr. Willow said to everyone as he divided the stack of paper into thirds. "You know, when I was your age, I had to take my math quizzes out in the snow in my bare feet."

"For real?" Simon asked.

"Yes, Simon. For *reeeaaal*," Mr. Willow said and handed him a short stack of papers. "And we didn't have paper. We had to use tree bark to write on. And we didn't have pens or pencils either."

"What did you do?" asked Simon, taking his share of the quizzes. I wasn't quite sure if Simon believed Mr. Willow or just wanted him to continue with the joke.

"We bit off the tips of our index fingers," Mr. Willow answered, opening his eyes wide and pulling his left index finger close to his mouth. "We'd write the answers with our own blood!"

Everybody thought this was funny.

Whenever we complained about something, Mr. Willow liked to exaggerate and make stuff up about how tough it was back in the old days. We were used to it.

There were nine tables in our class with three kids at each table. Rosie passed out the quizzes to the back row of three tables. I handled the middle row. And Simon took care of the front row closest to Mr. Willow's desk.

It only took a minute.

5

Well, it only took me and Rosie a minute. When we were done, Rosie said, "Molly."

I turned my head toward her. She pointed at Simon.

And that's when the trouble started.

SIMON WAS STILL at his first table. He hadn't handed out a single quiz.

He was standing in front of Lizzy Jacobsen at Table 7. Simon had one of the math quizzes in his right hand. And he was sort of shaking it at her.

Not in a mean way. It was more like in a frustrated way—like he couldn't let go of it or something. He shook his hand harder, but the quiz stayed stuck there.

Finally, he used his left hand to peel the quiz loose and hand it to Lizzy.

Lizzy looked at it and said, "Gross."

Mr. Willow had not noticed any of this. His back was turned as he wrote today's schedule on the whiteboard.

TODAY'S SCHEDULE

1. MATH QUIZ (FUN, FUN, FUN!)
2. SCIENCE—PHOTOSYNTHESIS (HERE COMES THE SUN!)
3. SILENT READING TIME (YOU CHOOSE THE BOOK!)
4. LUNCH (MUNCH!)
5. RECESS (GO WILD!)
6. COMPOSITION (WRITE ON!)
7. ART (WHAT WILL YOU MAKE?!)
8. DISMISSAL

Once Lizzy had her paper, Simon handed a quiz to Billy Price.

I should say he *tried* to hand a quiz to Billy Price.

It didn't work out very well.

The same thing happened. Billy's quiz was stuck to Simon's right hand. He shook it at him, but it didn't come loose. He shook it harder and the paper rustled loudly.

"What is he doing?" I whispered to Rosie. We were back at Table 5 now. "Is he doing that on purpose?"

"I don't think so."

Simon shook it harder—and it rustled even louder.

This got Mr. Willow's attention. He turned around.

"Uh-oh," Rosie said.

Simon shoved his right hand and the quiz toward Billy.

"Just take it," Simon said. I think he knew that Mr. Willow was looking now. *Everybody* was looking.

Billy grabbed the edge of the paper and pulled.

Riiiiiip!

Billy got half of his quiz.

The other half was still stuck to Simon's hand.

"Simon, what is going on?" Mr. Willow

asked loudly. It wasn't a mean voice, but it sure wasn't friendly either.

Simon didn't answer. He just held his hand palm out toward Mr. Willow, showing him that one-half of Billy's math quiz was stuck there. And now we could all see that there were splotches of brown stuff on Simon's hand.

"What is that?" Mr. Willow asked. "On your hand?"

"Sap."

"Sap?"

"Yeah," Simon answered and pushed his hand closer so Mr. Willow could see better. "Like from a tree."

"I know what sap is, Simon," Mr. Willow said and closed his eyes for two seconds. "I'm just wondering why it's on your hands. And, more importantly, why it's tearing my quizzes."

"It's a long story," Simon answered and tried to peel the rest of the paper off with his other hand. "See, this morning I was at Picasso Park and—"

"Stop," Mr. Willow

said and shook his head. He wasn't mad or anything. It just looked like he wanted to get the school day started. "Go wash your hands."

"It's super sticky," Simon said. "I washed them, like, a million times already."

"Try a million more," Mr. Willow said as he took the quizzes from Simon and began to pass the rest of them out.

Simon went to the boys' bathroom.

When Simon finally told us the whole story, Rosie and I knew it was bad news.

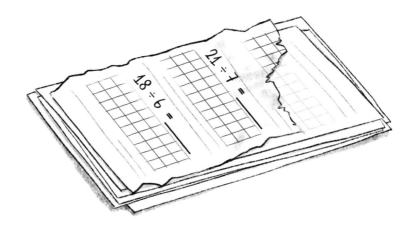

GREAT NEWS!
YOU'VE ALREADY
READ TWO CHAPTERS,
FOURTEEN PAGES,
AND 957 WORDS.

CHAPTER THREE

SUPER MAD

SIMON COULDN'T TELL us about the tree sap on his hands during science. That's because the three of us were in different groups.

At the beginning of science, each group took a big oak tree leaf that Mr. Willow had collected that morning. We put the leaf in a shallow bowl of water on the windowsill in the sunshine.

Then Mr. Willow talked for a long time about how plants convert the sun's light energy into oxygen and release it.

At the end of science period, we observed our leaves—and they had tiny bubbles around their edges. That was oxygen being released. It was pretty cool.

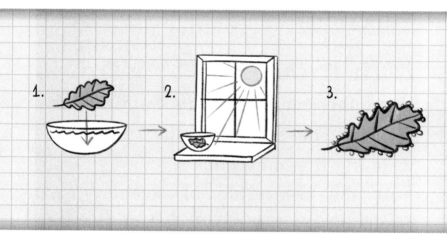

We got our chance to talk to Simon during silent reading time. He sat in the middle of Table 5. That way when he whispered, Rosie and I could both hear him.

We held our books up in front of our faces so Mr. Willow wouldn't see us talking.

We whispered the whole time.

Rosie asked, "What's the deal with the tree sap on your hands?"

"I was at Picasso Park yesterday," Simon said. You could tell something was bothering him a lot. "And Max Brutus was there too. He was practicing soccer— just juggling and taking shots at the net. I can't believe how hard that dude can kick. It's like a rocket!"

Rosie and I knew who Max Brutus was: He was the biggest and strongest kid in our grade. He always won at dodgeball—and everything else—in gym. He even knocked Hector Cruz over with a dodgeball throw once.

"So how does Max being at the park lead to you getting tree sap all over your hands?" asked Rosie.

"I asked him if I could practice with him," Simon replied. "And he said yes.

I was surprised because he's kind of a grumpy guy, you know? But anyway, we each took turns in goal. We took five shots each and then switched. He's really good—and strong. He kicks like a high schooler."

I peeked over my book. Mr. Willow was reading at his desk—and not looking at us. I ducked my head back down and asked, "What about the tree sap?"

"I'm getting to that part," Simon said.

TABLE
5

"After a little while, Max had to go home. And I asked him if I could keep playing with his soccer ball. It's a really nice one. It's a replica of the ball they used when the World Cup was here in the United States. It looks like the real thing!"

"Did he say yes?" Rosie asked.

Simon nodded and said, "As long as I bring it back to him today."

I asked, "So what happened?"

"I was punting it real high, just messing around," Simon said. You could tell this was when something bad happened. "You know I can kick good too. And I—"

Simon stopped then. It was like he didn't want to talk anymore.

"You what?" asked Rosie.

"I accidentally kicked it into the top of a really tall tree," Simon said. "That really big pine tree by the basketball court. And it got stuck."

"Oh no," I said. I knew that tree. It was the tallest tree in Picasso Park.

Simon squeezed his eyes shut and said, "He's going to be super mad."

"You're right," somebody said. "He is going to be super mad."

It wasn't Rosie who said it. Or me. Or Simon.

It was Mr. Willow.

CHAPTER FOUR

A TALL TREE AND TATER TOTS

MR. WILLOW WASN'T talking about Max Brutus being super mad that Simon got his ball stuck in a tree. He was talking about himself being super mad because we were talking. In class. Again.

He stood behind our table. He looked really tall standing over us like that.

"Rosie," he said. "Can you look at the whiteboard and tell me what number three says on today's schedule?"

"It says 'Silent reading time.'"

"And Molly," he said, turning his head to stare at me. "Are the three of you *silent*?"

"No, sir."

"And Simon," Mr. Willow said, glaring at him now. "Are the three of you *reading*?"

"Not exactly."

He pointed at each of us and then at our books. Then he growled. It wasn't a funny, playful growl. It was more like an I-better-not-have-to-tell-you-again growl.

So we didn't talk—until lunch.

We found a table to ourselves. For lunch, we had a grilled cheese sandwich, tater tots, an orange, and a brownie. It was a really good lunch for me. That's because the grilled cheese sandwich was cut in two—and I only eat things in even numbers. And there were eight tater tots, so I didn't have to give any to Simon or Rosie—it was already an even number.

And Simon's favorite dessert is brownies. So I looked forward to giving him mine.

"So you kicked Max's special World Cup soccer ball into a tree?" Rosie asked, reminding us where we were in the conversation.

"Not just *any* tree," Simon said. "The tallest tree in Picasso Park."

"And that's how you got sap on your hands?" I asked. "You tried to climb the tree?"

"I *did* climb it this morning," Simon said, tossing three tater tots in his mouth. "I thought about it all night. But this morning I couldn't climb high enough. That dumb ball is almost at the top. I got as high as I could, but I could feel the tree trunk start to bend with my weight. I got kind of scared and had to stop."

"Simon!" Rosie exclaimed. "I know that tree! You can't climb that high. It's totally dangerous!"

"Yeah," Simon said and squeezed his little paper cup of ketchup into his mouth.

27

"But it'sh not as dangeroush ash not giving Max hish ball back."

"Wait," Rosie said, shaking her head. "Did you just put your tater tots in your mouth and then the ketchup after?"

Simon nodded.

"You don't dip them in the ketchup and *then* eat them?" I asked.

"Not anymore," Simon said. He had swallowed it all now. "Smart, right?"

Rosie asked, "How is it smart?"

"It totally saves time," Simon said. And to demonstrate, he shoved four more tots into his mouth and squeezed the rest of his ketchup in. He chewed and mumbled, "It'sh way more efficientsh."

"It's way more *something*," Rosie said and laughed.

And then she stopped laughing.

Someone was standing over us again.

CHAPTER FIVE

HERE COMES MAX

THIS TIME, IT wasn't Mr. Willow standing over us.

It was Max Brutus. He was wearing his red-and-black Evanston Eagles soccer jersey. It was stretched tight around his biceps. He's a big dude.

"Umm," Simon said, looking up at him. "Hi, Max. How's it going?"

"Bowman," Max said. He only calls his close friends by their first names. For everybody else, Max only uses last names. And Simon's last name is Bowman. "Do you have my—"

"Hey, Max!" Simon interrupted. He was obviously trying to keep Max from asking about his World Cup soccer ball. "I was just showing Molly and Rosie a new way I eat tater tots! Check it out!"

Simon grabbed four tater tots—two off my tray and two off Rosie's—and shoved them into his mouth. He grabbed my ketchup cup and squeezed it in after the tots. Then he looked up at Max, chewing and smiling.

Max sort of squeezed his left eye shut slightly and scrunched his mouth over to one side. He said, "Umm. That's great. Did you bring—"

To help Simon, Rosie interrupted.

"Max, can I ask you a question?" she said quickly.

Max turned to her.

"Yeah, I guess," he answered. "I really just wanted to get—"

"Great, thanks," Rosie said even faster, not allowing Max to finish. "I was just wondering. If you were a car, what kind of car would you be?"

"Huh?"

"If you were a car, what kind of car would you be?" Rosie repeated. I had never heard her talk so quickly—and her voice was a little higher too. "You can pick anything. An old-fashioned car, a new one, whatever. You can even choose a pickup truck if you want. Your options are wide open. Whatever!"

"Why do you want to—"

"I'll use myself as an example," Rosie continued rapidly. "I would choose a Volkswagen Beetle. A green one! Because I'm interested in bugs. The study of bugs is called entomology! Isn't that an interesting word? Like, it should be bugology, don't you think? That would be way better. Anyway, what kind of car would you be?"

Max looked confused. After five seconds, he said, "I guess I'd be a van. We have a red van and use it to go camping."

"Awesome!" Rosie said with great enthusiasm. "That's a great choice."

"Umm, thanks," Max said and shook his head a little. He turned back to Simon.

"So, Bowman, where's my—"

It was my turn.

"Oranges are one of my favorite fruits, Max!" I shouted.

He yanked his head toward me and said, "What?"

"Oranges are my favorite fruit!" I said, lowering my voice. I realized that I had just shouted. "That's because they're orange on the inside and orange on the outside. I love that!"

"Okay."

"And look at this!" I said and pointed down at my lunch tray. I had separated my orange into its sections. "There's ten slices. An even number! Isn't that the best? The absolute best?!"

"I guess."

Then Max shook his head again. I think he might have been trying to shake off the past three minutes of conversation. He stared down at Simon.

"Bowman, where's my ball?"

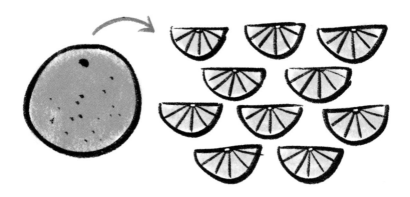

UH-OH! WHAT DO YOU THINK WILL HAPPEN NEXT?

CHAPTER SIX

THIS IS BAD

"EXCUSE ME?" SIMON answered. I knew he didn't say that because he didn't *hear* Max. He said that because he didn't know how to *answer* Max. "Um, what?"

"I said, where's my ball?" Max said.

Then Simon opened his eyes really wide, like he was in absolute shock. He slapped his forehead hard.

"Gosh *darn* it!" Simon exclaimed. "I totally forgot it. Sorry."

Max stared at Simon for a couple of seconds. It wasn't a mean stare. It was more like a disappointed stare. Max wasn't intimidating because he wasn't nice, he was intimidating because he was huge. Like, you know, massive.

"It's all right, Bowman," he said after that two-second stare down. "But we're playing for the championship at five o'clock at Picasso Park. And it's my lucky ball. Bring it to me there."

"Okay," Simon said quickly and nodded his head fast. "I'll bring it."

Max seemed satisfied with that, but he wanted to make certain. He asked, "You'll bring it, right?"

"Right," Simon replied. "Five o'clock. Got it."

"For sure?"

"For sure."

Max left.

Simon waited until Max was on the other side of the cafeteria, then he said, "You guys, what am I going to do?"

It was a totally bad situation. Max's favorite World Cup soccer ball was stuck in the top of Picasso Park's tallest tree. The tree was way too high—and way too flimsy at the top—to climb. It would be dangerous for sure.

"Maybe it will be really windy this afternoon," I said, trying to make Simon feel better. "Maybe we'll go to Picasso Park after school and the ball will just be there at the foot of the tree waiting for you."

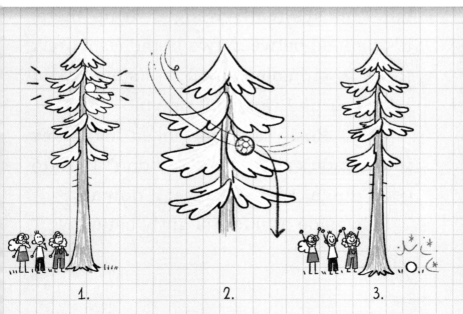

1.   2.   3.

"Yeah, maybe," Simon said. He didn't really believe that was possible, I could tell. "But it's really wedged in up there. It's trapped between two branches. I don't think it will come down on its own. And I don't think I can get it down."

"Hey," Rosie said and poked her elbow into Simon's shoulder. "*You* don't have to get it down. *We* have to get it down."

This made him feel slightly better.

"We'll go straight to the park after school," I told him.

"We have to figure it out fast," Rosie said. "We'll only have about an hour before Max gets there for his game."

Simon looked nervous.

"Here," I said and handed my brownie to Simon to make him feel better. "You can have it. I know it's your favorite."

"No, thanks," Simon said. "I'm not hungry."

Rosie looked at me. This wasn't a good sign. We both knew it. If Simon didn't want to eat my brownie, he was feeling bad. Really bad.

Simon looked around to make sure nobody could hear him but us. "Can I ask you guys a question?"

We both nodded.

"Do you think Max shaves?"

CHAPTER SEVEN

WE'LL GET A CAT!

WE DIDN'T GO straight to Picasso Park after school. We decided to go to Simon's house first. We thought there might be something in his garage that we could use to get the ball down. On the way, we tried to think of ways to get it out.

"Fire trucks have really tall ladders," Simon said as we left school and reached the sidewalk. "Maybe we could use one of those."

"How are we going to get a fire truck?" I asked.

"We'll get a cat!" Simon said quickly.

"Why?" asked Rosie.

"Sometimes firefighters rescue cats that get stuck in trees," Simon said. He liked this idea. He got that hazy look in his eyes and started to talk faster. "We'll get a cat and take it to the tree! It will climb up and get totally stuck!"

"Then what?" I asked.

"Then we'll call 911," Simon answered. His eyes were kind of bulged out with excitement. "And we'll be like, 'Help! Our cat is trapped in a tree! Can you bring your truck with a big ladder and get her out?! Oh, and by the way, there happens to be a soccer ball up there too.

Would you mind getting that down while you're up there?' That might work."

Rosie had her doubts.

"None of us have a cat," Rosie said. "So we'd have to find one. Then we'd have to hope it gets stuck. And what if there's an actual fire somewhere? We don't want to take firefighters away from their real job."

"Okay, forget the cat," Simon said, already admitting that part of his plan wouldn't work. "But we can still use the idea!"

"How?" I asked.

"We'll start an actual fire!" Simon exclaimed. "In the tree itself! If the tree is burning, firefighters have to come! Heck, the soccer ball might fall out as the branches burn and break!"

"Simon!" Rosie and I exclaimed.

"What?"

"We can't start a fire on purpose!" Rosie said. "It's against the law! It's dangerous! And the soccer ball would probably catch on fire too. Then you'd have to give Max a pile of ashes instead of his ball. I don't think he'd like that very much."

You could tell Simon knew Rosie was right.

"Okay, okay," he said as we turned into his driveway. "Not a good idea."

"Maybe we'll find something in your garage." I said.

We knew all about Simon's garage. We had cleaned and organized it a few months before to help Simon after he got in trouble for getting way too excited about Cocoa Puffs cereal. It's a long story.

We stood in the middle of the

garage and then turned slowly around. There was a lot of stuff. We thought of three ideas.

"We could just throw stuff at it and knock it down," I suggested.

So we got a football and three Frisbees.

"If we can find something long and skinny, we could poke it out," Rosie said.

So we got a bunch of skinny white PVC pipes and connectors. Simon said he had used that stuff to make forts when he was little.

"We could shake the tree," Simon said. "You know, like, really hard."

We didn't need anything from the garage for that.

And then we loaded everything into Simon's red wagon and went to Picasso Park.

CHAPTER EIGHT

I'M A GOOD KICKER

PICASSO PARK IS really big. It's got all kinds of stuff—two baseball diamonds, a fishing pond, a basketball court, a big playground, a walking trail with ten exercise stations, three soccer fields, and four tennis courts.

The tree was by the basketball court on the other side of the park. We saw four people on the way.

First, we saw my mom. For real.

She was at the first exercise station on the walking trail. She was using her stretchy elastic band. It was wrapped around a pole and she pulled on it and grunted. When she saw us, she stopped.

"What are . . . you three . . . up to?" Mom asked after saying hello to Simon and Rosie. She panted a little bit between words. "And what . . . are you doing . . . with all . . . that stuff?"

"We have to get a ball out of a tree," I answered.

"Balls can . . . grow . . . on trees?" Mom asked. She was joking.

But Simon didn't know she was joking.

"I kicked it up into the big pine tree by the basketball court," he said. "Rosie and Molly are going to help me get it out."

"I see," Mom said and nodded. She didn't care that Simon didn't get her joke. She started to pull on her elastic band again. "Molly, when I finish the trail . . . it's time . . . to go home. It's a school night."

We also passed Mr. Garcia at the fishing pond. He fishes there all the time. He said he hadn't caught anything yet.

And there were two teenagers playing tennis.

Then we got to the basketball court— and the tree.

"It's taller than I thought," Rosie said, stretching her neck to look up at the top. "It's huge."

"How did you kick Max's soccer ball all the way up there?" I asked.

"I'm a good kicker, I guess," Simon said and shrugged.

"You must be."

"Come on," Rosie said. Her eyes were squinted and her lips were squeezed tight. "Let's get started."

We tried the white PVC pipes first. It took a long time to connect them all. We had to squeeze the pipes into the connectors really tightly— and sometimes they were a little too loose and sometimes they were a little too tight.

But when we did finish, the result was excellent. The final pipe was almost as long as the basketball court.

"This will totally reach the ball!" Simon yelled from the far end of the long pipe. He was excited that our first idea could work. "Let's lift it up!"

"Okay!" Rosie called. She and I were at the other end. We had just attached the final piece. Rosie seemed confident too.

Rosie's Wicked Ride

Just to me, she said, "This is going to be easier than I thought."

Then we lifted the super long pipe.

We found out that it wasn't going to be easier than we thought. We also found out we were running out of time.

Mom was already doing push-ups at station three of the exercise trail. And we saw someone else arrive at the park—someone we really didn't want to see.

CHAPTER NINE

STAY TOGETHER, STAY TOGETHER

WE SAW ONE of Max's teammates heading toward the soccer fields. It wasn't Max. This player was too small to be Max. But it was still a totally bad sign.

"It's not time for the game yet!" Simon exclaimed. "What's he doing here?!"

"He probably got here early to warm up," Rosie said.

"What if Max gets here early?!" Simon asked with wide-open eyes.

Rosie and I didn't answer. We just picked up the pipe as fast as we could.

We had lots of trouble with it.

First, when we started to stand it up, the pipe came apart at three different connectors. We put it back together, tried again, and it came loose at two other connectors.

"Okay, wait," Rosie said after our second attempt. She had a plan. "Let's do this differently. I'll stay at this end— the bottom. Molly, you stand about a third of the way up. And Simon, you go between Molly and the far end.

By slowly lifting it together, there will be less strain in the middle and I think we can stand it up."

I went to my spot.

And Simon went to his.

"Okay," Rosie called to us. "One, two—"

But Rosie stopped counting. She looked at Simon. And so did I.

He was not grasping the pipe and getting ready to lift it. He stood over the pipe with his eyes closed. His two index fingers were pressed gently into the sides of his head. Rosie and I had never seen him do something like this before. We hustled toward him.

When we got there, I whispered, "Simon?"

It just seemed like I should whisper. I don't know why.

"*Shh*," he whispered back.

Rosie asked softly, "What are you doing?"

"I'm using the Force," Simon said and slowly swayed his head back and forth like he was in a trance. "I am becoming one with the pipe. This *has* to work."

"What?!" Rosie asked, this time not as softly.

"I'm surrounding the pipe with positive

energy," Simon said, still whispering and swaying. He chanted, "Stay together, stay together, stay together."

Then Simon opened his eyes and said, "It's ready now."

"Are you crazy?" Rosie said and laughed.

Simon said, "Maybe. But I'll try anything to get Max's ball back."

After that, we got the pipe to stand up on the first try. Simon said it was the Force that did it, but he was just kidding. We knew it was the *way* we did it that kept the pipe together.

We moved slowly and carefully to the tree—and then began to lean the pipe toward Max's World Cup soccer ball.

It did not work. Not even close. And we tried four times.

The pipe was too long and flimsy and impossible to control. It broke apart each time. We had to put it back together and get it upright again.

And again.

And again.

On the fourth try, the top end of the pipe snagged in some branches. When we pulled on it, the whole thing broke again.

Rosie said, "I think we better try something else."

Simon and I agreed.

Mom was at exercise station six. And two more of Max's teammates were walking toward the soccer field.

We were running out of time.

CHAPTER TEN

SMACK!

"LET'S SHAKE IT out!" Simon said quickly.

Rosie looked at the massive tree trunk— then she looked at me. I could tell she didn't think we could shake Max's soccer ball loose. But we thought it might make Simon feel better to give it a try.

The three of us ducked under some of the lower branches and pressed our palms against the bark.

"On your mark! Get set!" Simon said loudly. "Go!"

We pushed on the trunk.

It didn't move an inch. There was no way it would work.

"All we have left is to throw stuff at it," I said. I pointed at my mom. She was jogging toward the tenth station— jumping jacks.

"We better go fast. Mom's going to be done soon."

"And there are five soccer players now," Simon said after jerking his head toward the field. He was worried. "Max could get here any minute!"

We got the three Frisbees and football.

We tried the Frisbees first. Some of our throws got pretty close, but none of them actually hit Max's soccer ball. And it took a lot of time to retrieve our Frisbees after

every throw.
It wasn't like
the tree threw
them back
to us.

Simon picked
up the football.

"Might as well try this," he said.
He sounded defeated.

Simon threw it three times—
and missed every time. Rosie and I
watched as Simon leaned back and
threw the football as hard as he could a
fourth time. It was a way better throw.

"That looks good!" Rosie said when it
was halfway up. "It's got a chance!"

Smack!

Simon's football hit Max's soccer ball
right in the middle. Hard too.

"Yes!" Simon screamed.

We watched the football tumble down through the big pine tree's branches and hit the ground.

Then we watched for the soccer ball.

But it did not come down.

It was still up there.

It looked like it was wedged even deeper between those two branches.

"Ugh!" Simon said, realizing what had happened. "Are you kidding me? Seriously?! I think it's *more* stuck!"

Then somebody yelled.

It wasn't Simon.

Or Rosie.

Or me.

It was Mom.

"Leaving in three minutes!" she called from exercise station number ten. She was now using her elastic band to stretch. She always did that for a few minutes after a workout.

We gathered everything—the white PVC pipes, connectors, three Frisbees, and the football. When we had everything, Simon, Rosie, and I stood together and stared up at Max's soccer ball.

"I can't believe I made the perfect football throw—and pushed it *deeper*. It got *more* stuck," Simon groaned and turned nervously toward the soccer field. "I'll tell Max the truth when he gets here."

Rosie's head twitched right then.

"Wait a minute," she whispered. "Wait a minute."

Simon and I watched. We both wanted to see Rosie do something—something very specific.

And she did it.

Rosie started to twirl her hair.

"I got it," she said. "I think I've got it."

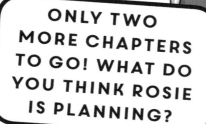

ONLY TWO MORE CHAPTERS TO GO! WHAT DO YOU THINK ROSIE IS PLANNING?

CHAPTER ELEVEN

PUSH
AND PULL

ROSIE SNAPPED HER head toward Simon.

She asked, "What did you just say?"

"I pushed it deeper."

"*That's* what we're doing wrong," Rosie said, looking at me and Simon. "We've been trying to *push* the ball—with the long pipe, the Frisbees, and the football."

We didn't know what she was talking about, but she explained it.

"We don't need to *push* the *ball*," Rosie said and smiled. "We need to *pull* the *branch*."

It made sense to me then, but I wanted to make sure. I asked, "We pull the lower branch out of the way?"

Simon added, "And the ball falls out?"

"And the ball falls out!" Rosie answered proudly.

"But, Rosie," Simon asked, "how do we do that?"

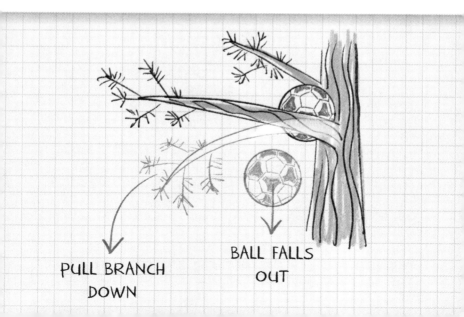

PULL BRANCH
DOWN

BALL FALLS
OUT

"We need three things," Rosie said. I could tell that she was super confident in her idea. "And all three of them are right here at the park!"

Rosie explained her idea. Then the three of us all ran in different directions.

Simon ran toward Mr. Garcia at the fishing pond.

Rosie ran to the tennis courts.

And I ran toward Mom.

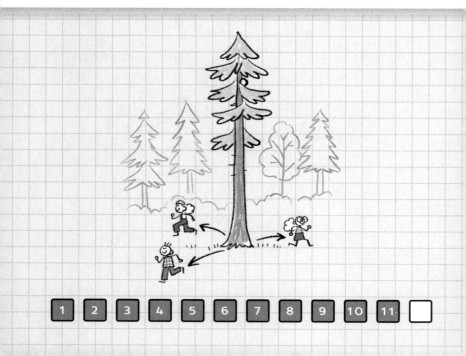

CHAPTER TWELVE

PULLING, BRACING, ZOOMING

THE TEENAGERS GAVE Rosie a tennis ball.

Simon brought back a spool of fishing line and said, "Mr. Garcia told me to keep it. He's got plenty."

I brought back Mom's stretchy exercise band.

"What do we do first?" Simon asked.

"We have to attach the fishing line to the tennis ball," Rosie said.

We wrapped that fishing line around the ball, like, a bajillion times. We wove it under and over and around the ball in every direction. When we were done, you could hardly see the ball at all.

"What's next?" I asked.

Rosie answered, "We unwind the spool all the way to the end."

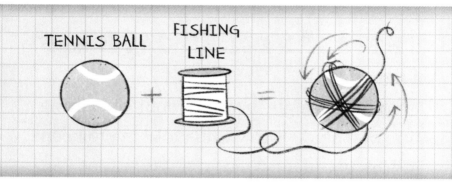

TENNIS BALL   FISHING LINE

The end of the fishing line was attached to the spool with a piece of tape. We peeled it off the spool. The fishing line was really thin, strong, and light.

"It's slingshot time!" Simon yelled.

Rosie looked at me and nodded real fast toward the parking lot near the soccer field. Max was getting out of his red van. We didn't tell Simon.

Rosie and I each stepped inside one end of Mom's long exercise band. It formed a loop around us. We stepped apart until it was tight enough to not fall down, but loose enough that Simon could pull on it real hard.

And that's what he did. He placed the
tennis ball against the stretchy band.

And pulled.

Rosie and I braced ourselves, digging
our feet into the grass.

Simon pulled.

We braced.

Simon bent down, closed one eye,
and drew an imaginary line between
the tennis ball in our giant homemade

slingshot—and the soccer ball up in the tree.

My legs were getting wobbly. Rosie's were too. I could see them trembling.

Simon closed both his eyes for one second, opened them—and let go.

With fishing line trailing behind it, the tennis ball zoomed up toward the top of the tree.

"Come on," Simon whispered. "Come on!"

It was a perfect shot.

The tennis ball soared toward Max's soccer ball. It bounced against the branch above the ball, fell back and bounced against the branch below it. Then it wrapped around that lower branch a couple of times.

The tennis ball hung and swung there. The trailing fishing line hung there too.

"Yes!" Simon yelled.

Rosie and I stepped out of the exercise band—and looked to the soccer field.

Max was jogging toward us.

The three of us raced to the tree. We took hold of the hanging fishing line—and yanked on it.

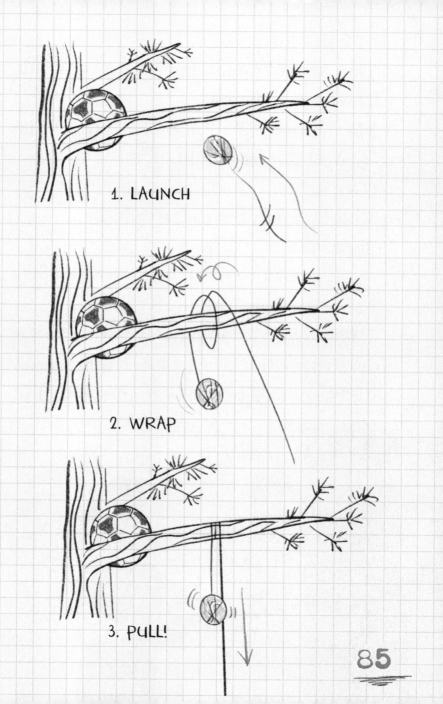

1. LAUNCH

2. WRAP

3. PULL!

85

That lower branch moved.

The leaves rustled.

Max's soccer ball tumbled out of the tree. And Simon caught it.

"Got it!" he yelled.

And then someone else yelled.

It was Max.

"Bowman!"

Simon turned around.

"Hey, Max!" Simon exclaimed. He tossed the ball to Max. "Here's your lucky ball!" Max caught it. He spun the ball in

his hands and sort of examined it. Then he smiled.

"Thanks, Simon," Max said and turned toward the soccer field. It was almost game time.

"Good luck in the game!" Simon called as Max hurried away. Then in a lower voice he talked to Rosie and me. "Did you hear that?"

"What?" Rosie asked.

"He didn't call me 'Bowman,'" Simon answered and smiled. "He called me 'Simon.'"

CONGRATULATIONS!

You've read **12** chapters,

87 pages,

and **5,980** words!

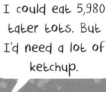

You read even better than Max plays soccer!

5,980 feet is almost halfway up Mount Fuji in Japan.

I could eat 5,980 tater tots. But I'd need a lot of ketchup.

Fun and Games!

THINK

Think of a different way to get Max's soccer ball out of the tree. Where would it rank compared to the plans devised by Molly, Rosie, and Simon? Better than all of them? Worse? In the middle? Can you draw a picture of your plan?

FEEL

Simon is really worried that Max will be mad at him. When was the last time you thought someone might be mad at you? What happened? Was it kind of bad? Or did everything turn out okay?

ACT

In this book, Molly explains how she likes to eat fruit in a certain way. And Simon eats tater tots in a *totally* unique way. What about you? Can you make your own snack and eat it in a new, safe, and fun way?